Max In India

Max In India

By Adam Whitmore
Illustrated by Janice Poltrick Donato

Silver Burdett Company
Morristown, New Jersey and Agincourt, Ontario

Library of Congress Cataloging in Publication Data
Whitmore, Adam.
Max in India.
Summary: Max the cat's search for his missing tail
takes him to India, where he befriends a tiger
and has several dangerous adventures.
[1. Cats—Fiction. 2. Tail—Fiction.
3. Tigers—Fiction. 4. India—Fiction]
I. Donato, Janice Poltrick, ill. II. Title.
PZ7.W5977Maw 1986 [Fic] 86-6451
ISBN 0-382-09245-7

Copyright © 1986 by Maxcat Inc
Published in the United States
in 1986 by Silver Burdett Company,
Morristown, New Jersey

Published simultaneously in Canada by
GLC/Silver Burdett Publishers

Produced by Acacia House Publishing Services Ltd

Printed in Spain by H. Fournier, S.A.

MAX is a big marmalade cat
with a fine round head, long bushy whiskers,
and big furry paws.
He is a very handsome cat, but one thing is wrong.
He has no tail.
Because he looks different from the other cats,
none of them will play with him.
Max sets out to find his tail,
and get it back from whoever has taken it,
so the other cats will be his friends.
He searches all over London, where he lives,
and when he does not find it
he sneaks aboard a flight to America.
He searches everywhere
until, in San Francisco, he is captured by a sailor
and taken on board ship.

MAX IN INDIA

Max was at sea in the ship for five weeks, and he thought this was the happiest time of his life so far.

He ate very well. The ship's cook, who had brought him on board in a sack, gave him two meals a day. Sometimes it was steak, cooked rare, the way Max liked it. And there was always vanilla or coffee ice cream. Max loved both kinds.

Max had a lot of healthy exercise, too. He caught all the rats that the cook had wanted cleared from the ship. That took two weeks. When all the rats were gone, Max spent his days lying on the deck in the hot, bright sun. He stretched out on his back with his paws folded on his chest, just as he used to do at home.

But best of all, there were no other cats around to make fun of him for not having a tail. Still, Max looked forward to the day when the ship would reach a port. Then he could go ashore and start searching for his tail again.

One day Max found all the sailors who were on deck standing at the rail, pointing into the distance. He went to see where they were looking. Far away, on the very edge of the sea, was a long white line that looked hazy. It grew clearer, though, as the ship moved closer to it. The sailors all said it was land.

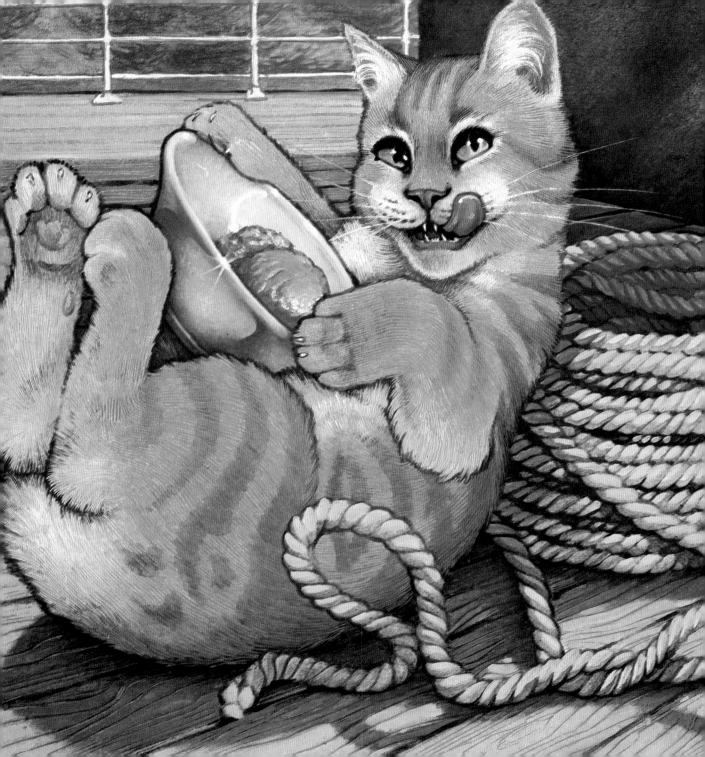

Soon, Max could see that they were heading for a big city. There were many other ships moving in and out of the port. As soon as Max's ship tied up beside the dock, the sailors lowered a gangplank. Some of the men who were working there came on board to help unload the cargo. Most of them had bare feet. Some had cloths wrapped around their heads.

When Max saw that all the sailors were too busy to

notice him, he bounded down the gangplank onto the dock. Then he ran down an alley between two ware-houses.

There he came face to face with the thinnest, hungriest-looking cat he had ever seen. It was rusty black, and its ribs and shoulder bones showed through its rumpled fur.

"Hello," Max said. "Where am I? What city is this?"

"Calcutta," the thin cat said.

"That's in India, isn't it?" Max remembered from a TV film.

"Yes," said the thin cat. "Where have you come from?"

"England. Then America. I just got off a ship from San Francisco."

"If I were you, I'd get back on it," the thin cat sighed, "or you'll soon be as thin as I am." He sounded tired and sad.

"Why don't you find something to eat?" Max said.

"I wish I could. I lived with a family once. A long time ago, now, and far from here. But I was a wanderer and now I'm old. In this part of Calcutta, many people are poor and it's hard to find food, even to hunt for it at my age."

"I have to stay here for a while anyway," Max said. "I have to look for my tail."

"Why?"

"Because I haven't got one," said Max. "Don't you think I look funny?"

"When you're old and hungry like me, nothing seems funny," the thin cat said. "If I could trade you my tail for some food, or to be young again, I'd do it now. A tail's not important."

"It is to me," Max said, but before he walked on, he told the thin cat how to find the ship he'd come from. Maybe the cook would give him some food.

Max felt sad about that cat. He saw other thin cats that day, too, though, as he walked through the city streets and the noisy street markets. Calcutta was such a crowded place that Max decided to move on.

So he walked very fast, and sometimes even ran,

though it was hot and he was thirsty. Soon he found himself alone on a dusty country road. He had been walking for about an hour, when something he saw in the tall grass beside it made him stop short.

It was a wonderful tail: long and thick, with a pattern of yellow and black stripes. Max imagined how grand he would look with a tail like that as he walked over to where it was lying, gripped it in both front paws, and tugged hard.

But the tail did not move.

Max tugged again, harder.

The tail twitched, just once, up and down, and it tossed Max back onto the road. Then, the deepest voice he had ever heard said, "Who's playing games when I'm trying to sleep?"

Max picked himself up quickly. As he was shaking the dust from his coat, the tall grass parted, and a huge black and yellow head looked out, wide whiskers bristling, yellow eyes angry.

It was a tiger. *Max had tried to take a tiger's tail!* And, oh, such a *big* tiger!

"Are you the one who pulled my tail?" the tiger rumbled.

Making his own voice as deep as he could, Max said, "Yes, I'm the one." He thought the best thing to do then would be to run off down the dusty road as fast as he could. He also knew the tiger could catch him in one leap — and Max would be less than a mouthful of lunch for him.

But as soon as he heard Max's voice, the tiger stopped frowning and said, "I know your accent. Are you English?"

"Yes," said Max.

The tiger nodded. "I thought so." He stepped out of the tall grass then. "A lot of English people used to live in India, you know. I've always enjoyed their food, though it's not spicy like ours. Some of them used to picnic around here, and I interrupt picnics now and then. When I do, the same thing always happens. The people drive away in a hurry and leave their food for me. Only the other day, I had some delicious curried eggs." The tiger smiled with pleasure at the memory. "What's your name?" he asked.

"Max."

"Max, you may call me Rajah. What are you doing in India all on your own?"

"It's a long story," said Max. He was feeling much more comfortable now.

"I've got plenty of time." Rajah sat back on his haunches. "Tell me."

"I've come in a ship from America — from San Francisco, and I was in New York too, looking for something. Now I'm going to look all over India. Before I left home, I had looked everywhere in London too."

"What are you looking for?" asked Rajah.

"My tail. I haven't got one."

"I've noticed, Max. How did you lose it?"

"I don't know. I don't even remember when I had it. Someone took it when I was a kitten, I suppose. Now I want it back. I want other cats to stop making fun of me. Do *you* think I look funny, Rajah?"

"No. No, of course not," Rajah said quickly. He *did* think Max looked a little funny, but he wouldn't say so because he could see how troubled Max was about it. Besides, he believed that making fun of others was a poor way for a tiger or anyone else to behave. "Did you grab my tail because you thought it was yours?"

"Yes," Max said.

"You're very brave, little brother."

"I really want my tail, so the other cats will accept me and come play with me. Rajah, I get so lonely sometimes."

Rajah sat looking down at Max. "Yes," he rumbled. "Yes, I imagine you do." He stood up. "I'm going to help you look for your tail, Max. We belong to the same family, you and I, and I must help you. You don't know India. It's a hard country  and I don't think you'd be able to survive alone. You need me.''

"It would be good to have a friend,'' Max said.

Smiling, Rajah patted him on the side of the head — and knocked him rolling in the dust.

"Ouch!'' Max got up. "Why did you do that?''

"Sorry, Max. That was supposed to be a friendly tap. Sometimes I forget how strong I am.'' Embarrassed because he had been so clumsy, Rajah pointed up the road. "Let's go.''

They walked many miles, day after day, across the

great central tableland of India, called the Deccan. They kept away from towns, and even villages.

Then one day, Max thought he had found his tail at last. He was walking along, a few paces ahead of Rajah, when he saw something just ahead. It was dark brown, with yellow stripes a bit like his own. It was just lying there, like a tail that had dropped off someone.

Max trotted forward to pick it up. But as he reached for it, it moved and turned. Then he saw it had a head, with bright little eyes and a tongue that flickered out at him. It was a snake.

Max stood completely still, watching the eyes that watched him.

Suddenly the road trembled as Rajah came galloping. He made a deep roar as he leaped over Max and landed ahead of him. With a sweep of his great front paw, Rajah broke the snake's back and sent it sailing high into the air. It landed far out in a field.

Very angry, Rajah turned on Max. "That was a

krait! It could have killed you!" He raised a paw to hit Max, then stopped. More quietly, he said, "I warned you about India. You stay with me from now on!"

"All right, Rajah — but it did look like a tail."

"You and your tail," Rajah smiled. "Come on, little brother."

Next day, when they were nearing a village, they heard the crack-crack of rifles firing, then men shouting.

"What is it?" Max said.

"The village people are hunting a tiger. When they lose too many cattle, the people go and hunt the tiger that killed them."

"Have you ever killed their cattle, Rajah?"

Rajah looked very innocent. "Of course not. Remember what I said? I only take food from picnics."

"I hope the people from this village know that, Rajah."

"So do I — but let's not wait to find out. We tigers all look the same to those people."

Max ran as fast as he could then — but Rajah had only to lope along to keep up with him.

They were on a track that twisted and curved

among the trees when suddenly three men rushed out just ahead and stood right on the track. All of them aimed rifles at Rajah and Max.

"Stop, Max!" Rajah snapped, and he picked Max up in his teeth, then leaped off the track with him and into the trees, just as the men fired.

They all missed, and so they fired again at the spot where Rajah had disappeared. But he got away.

Holding Max in his mouth, Rajah ran until they could no longer hear rifle shots. Now they were out of the trees and close to a narrow stream where Rajah stopped and set Max down.

"That was quite a ride, Rajah." Max was rubbing the back of his neck. "My mother used to carry me in her mouth like that, when I was a kitten. I'd forgotten about it until now."

"Where is your mother?"

"I don't know. I don't remember anything about my family. Why, Rajah?"

"You should go back to your family, Max — or at least to some other country. India is too dangerous for you. Go somewhere else and look for your tail."

"I don't want to, Rajah. I don't care about my tail now. Even if I haven't got a tail, you're my friend. I'll stay with you."

But the tiger knew it was too dangerous for Max to live in India. Rajah had to say something to make him leave. "I'm not your friend. I'm no different from the other cats. I think you look funny, too."

Max was shocked and hurt. "All right, then, I'll go." He turned away.

"How will you go?" Rajah called after him.

"I'll find a plane or a ship," Max called without looking back.

"You don't know the way. I'll show you."

Rajah led Max down beside the stream and away over some hills. Two days later, they came to an airport on the edge of a city.

"I'll leave you now, Max," Rajah said.

"Thank you for helping me all these weeks. And, Rajah," said Max, "we *are* friends, aren't we? You didn't mean what you said?"

"No, I didn't mean it. We're friends — but sometimes friends have to go different ways. You have to go and look for your tail."

Rajah reached out with a big front paw and closed it around one of Max's. They shook hands, then said goodbye.

Max watched the big tiger swing away down the dusty road. Then he turned and walked over the field to the airport. He would climb aboard a plane somehow and go wherever it took him — and he hoped he would at last find his tail.